First published 1988 by Walker Books Ltd, London
Text copyright © 1989, 1988 by Martin Bax
Illustrations copyright © 1988 by Michael Foreman

Library of Congress Cataloging-in-Publication Data
Bax, Martin.
Edmond went far away.
Summary: Edmond bids good-bye to all the animals on
the farm and goes exploring to the "far away" land just
over the hill.
[1. Farm life—Fiction] I. Foreman, Michael, ill.
II. Title .
PZ7. A3305Ed 1989   [E]   88-16324
ISBN 0-15-225105-7

Printed in Italy
First U.S. edition 1989
A B C D E

EDMOND WENT FAR AWAY

Written by

MARTIN BAX

Illustrated by

MICHAEL FOREMAN

Harcourt Brace Jovanovich, Publishers   *San Diego   New York   London*

Edmond's Home

Edmond lived on a farm. A dirt path led from the road, crossed in front of the farm, and ran on through the fields down the hill. If you turned right when you left the house you came to the pond. On the pond there were three white ducks. When Edmond came to the water's edge they turned from whatever they were doing and swam toward him. Sometimes Edmond gave them bread. The ducks and Edmond were good friends.

Right across from the house there was the big barn with the pigsty beside it. In the sty lived a huge, fat sow. She often had as many as twelve piglets with her. Just now she had none, but she was very, very fat. She lay on the ground and didn't get up when Edmond came to see her. She opened her eyes, looked at him, and grunted.

In the barn, in the deep straw, were the calves. Most were black and white, but there were a few brown ones as well. Although the calves did not say much, they looked at Edmond with big, wide-open eyes.

In the fields nearby were the cows, who came into the barn every evening to be milked and then went back out again for the night. Though they never said anything to him about it, Edmond thought they must feel cold out there all night. The big old brown horse called Ned also lived in their field. He was retired and didn't go out very often. Edmond gave Ned sugar.

All around the farmhouse, along the path, and between the barns lived the hens – brown ones. There was one big rooster that Edmond especially liked, although he stalked away crowing whenever Edmond approached. Some of the hens even followed the path as it went on downhill. If Edmond found them there he chased them back to the farm.

Down the path at the bottom of the hill was a grove
of great tall trees. Most of them were beech trees. You
could walk under them on hot days, and it was beautifully
cool. In the treetops lived the crows. They built big nests
up there. When the crows saw Edmond coming, they
flew out of their nests. They didn't come down to him,
but they shouted excitedly. Except for trips in the car
(which didn't count) the grove was the farthest from
home that Edmond had ever been.

Edmond Goes Away

One afternoon Edmond came out of the house and said to himself – he said it aloud, so that anyone could hear who wanted – "I am going to walk far away." He stamped both his feet on the ground to make sure his sandals were firmly buckled. He shook his arms to make sure they would swing well. He kicked and jumped up and down a few times to make sure his legs were in good shape for walking far away. Then he set off.

First, he went to the ducks. The ducks swam toward him. "Ducks," Edmond said, "I am going far away."

"Quack," said the ducks. "Quack-away."

Then Edmond went to the pigsty and said to the fat sow, "I am going far away."

"Oink," she said. "Oink-away."

Then Edmond went to the calves and told them, "I am going far away."

But the calves said nothing. They just opened their big eyes wider than ever and stared at Edmond.

So Edmond went to the gate of the cow field and said to them, "I am going far away."

"Moo, moowar moo-way," said the cows, and Ned the old horse echoed them, singing out, "Neigh, neigh-away."

Then Edmond set off down the path toward the grove. Three or four hens popped out of the hedge, and he stopped for a moment to shoo them back toward the house.

"Tchuck-away, tchuck-away, tchuck-away," they said as they pattered up the path. Edmond strode on down the hill, hoping that his friends the crows would talk to him when he got to the grove.

They didn't let him down. They had seen him coming and he had barely got under the branches of the trees when they came swarming out of their nests calling, "Cor, cor, cor."

Edmond put his head back and shouted up to them, "Crows, I am going far away – far away, crows."

And the crows heard him, and called back, "Cor, cor, cor-away, cor-away." They circled around with a lot of excited flapping and then slowly, one by one, settled back in the trees.

Edmond was in no hurry to leave the grove. He walked all around, patting a few trees with his hands. The beech trees had nice smooth bark, and he stood very close to one small tree to see if he could get his arms all around it. He just could. Then it was time to go.

"Good-bye, trees," Edmond whispered.

"Shsh, shsh," said the trees. "Ssh-away."

Beyond the grove the path went on downhill a little way. At the bottom it was quite boggy and the path had thick green grass on it. There were deep tracks full of water, where the tractor had been. Edmond stayed close to the fence and passed the marshy part without getting his feet wet. Then he climbed up the hill – on and on toward the top. He had seen the top of the hill many times, but he had never been there. Soon he would be. Soon he would be far away.

The Long March

The path up the hill, which Edmond had seen often from his bedroom window at home, had not looked very long, but it went on and on. As Edmond marched up it he began to wish he had someone with him. Then he thought that perhaps some of his friends from the farmyard were with him and he was leading a long line of them up the hill.

He thought that immediately behind him he would like to have old Ned the horse, because if he got tired Ned would offer him a ride. Behind the horse he would have several of the crows. The crows would be very noisy, but as he got farther and farther away he could send them ahead to spy out the land. Cows, he thought, would be useful because if he got thirsty he could have a drink of milk, and if some hens rode on the backs of the cows, perhaps one of them might lay an egg.

The calves couldn't give him any milk, but when they got to the top of the hill they would be such good look-outs. He would stand four of them, each one pointing in a different direction, and they could tell him if anyone was coming. He couldn't think what the sow would do, but he would like her to come anyway.

The three ducks would be good to have with him because they made so much noise. Edmond himself had been quite frightened by their noise at first. If he met someone he didn't like, he would tell the ducks to quack at him. Edmond made several loud quacks himself — not that there was anyone to hear at the moment, but the noise was satisfying. It made him feel that all his friends really *were* just behind him.

It occurred to Edmond that he could ask his friends from home to help him. Ten of his red-coated soldiers would be handy if any enemies showed up. And he could use his rocking horse in case old Ned got tired and wanted a rest. And, finally, he would have to have the black and white panda who shared his bed.

Edmond marched on and on. He had been climbing steadily up the hill when he suddenly realized he was very close to the top. His shadowy friends all disappeared. He was Edmond, all alone and going far away. He threw up his arms in excitement and ran on to the top of the hill.

Edmond looked down at the new country he could claim as his own. Away to his left stretched great yellow fields of wheat, waiting to be harvested. To his right there was a village nestling among trees, and he could see the tall tower of a church. Beyond, the land rose again and on top of that hill was something that looked just like a castle.

Best of all, right below him and not very far away, was

a lake. The lake ended in rushes on one side and beyond them were trees. On the other side, the lake had a steep bank, and a boat was tied up to it. On the lake itself there was a single swan swimming round and round, while among the rushes were green and brown ducks poking their beaks into the mud.

All this was Edmond's country. He wanted to hug it all. He had found it by going far away.

A Night Far Away

Edmond had been so excited at the sight of his new country that he had run a little way down the hill. Now he found he could no longer see the grove, the fields, the barn, or the farmhouse. He ran quickly back to the top of the hill and looked back the way he had come.

There was the farmhouse; he could see his bedroom window and one of his yellow curtains lazily flapping in the breeze. Then his eye caught another movement. A familiar figure was walking up the path toward him. It was his father.

Looking back toward his father, Edmond waved uncertainly. Then he turned into the New World and walked on ahead. He took the path down to the lake where the rushes grew. The ground got very boggy but there were still places to stand safely. Edmond pulled at the reeds. They were firmly rooted, but finally he got up a good long one that he held up like a sword as he walked on around the lake toward the boat.

Where the boat was moored, Edmond found the bank was propped up by some wooden boards that had been driven into the water. This meant you could walk right up to the edge of the lake. Lying down, he could lean over the edge and just get his hand into the water to make some waves to rock the boat.

Edmond got up, pulled on the rope that moored the boat, and, when it reached the bank, jumped in. In the boat were oars. He could just lift them, but they were too big for him to use.

When his father finally caught up with Edmond they rowed out to the center of the lake because Edmond wished to speak to the swan. But the swan bowed its head twice at them, very politely, and then swam away.

They moored the boat again and Edmond walked on around the lake, picking up wood that had collected at the edge. In his knapsack, Edmond's father had a frying pan and some sausages. They built a fire with the driftwood and ate sausages and baked beans.

By now it was quite dark and the moon had risen. Edmond was glad to find that his father had brought him his sleeping bag. Because their fire was a little up the hill from the lake, Edmond could snuggle down and look out over the water. Wreaths of mist spiraled up from the lake. They looked, Edmond thought, like ghostly people, but friendly ones because they came from his lake. As they grew bigger he saw that they had the faces of all the people he liked best – all the friends he had left at home when he had come far away.

Edmond Comes Home

When the bright sun shone into his eyes Edmond woke up. A breeze was blowing the last of the mist off the lake. The swan was up and swimming around again in endless circles. Edmond's father was sitting up against a rock, wrapped in a blanket. Edmond thought he might be asleep, but as soon as he moved, his father opened his eyes and smiled at him.

Edmond slid out of his sleeping bag, pulled on his sandals, stood up, and looked around. The ducks remained in the reeds, but the swan rose halfway out of the water and shook its wings as if it were going to fly off. Instead it settled back into the water and glided toward Edmond, bowing good-bye. Edmond noticed that there were crows in the trees by the lake. Next time he would go over and talk to them.

Edmond's father seemed sleepy. So Edmond put the frying pan back into the knapsack and stuffed his sleeping bag in beside it. He pointed up the hill and his father nodded, smiling at him but saying nothing. Edmond turned and waved good-bye to the swan and to the ducks who were just emerging from the reeds. Then he waved to his father and started up the hill.

Edmond wondered if his home would look exactly the same when he got to the top of the hill. Perhaps during the night the whole place had changed. Farm, barn, grove, crows, calves, cows, sow, horse, and even ducks — all might have disappeared. In their place might be a huge town with big blocks of houses built of concrete. Edmond couldn't wait to reach the top of the hill.

He shut his eyes and slowed down for the last three or four steps. When he could feel he was at the very top, he took several deep breaths and then opened his eyes. It was still all there. The farm looked the same, although his bedroom window had been shut so the yellow curtain wasn't flapping. The barn still stood solid and square. In the field by the house were the cows and Ned. Ned was still there; he had not been far away.

Edmond ran down to the grove. While he had been away the leaves seemed to have grown greener and brighter. He rushed in among the trees and ran up to the small one. It was even smaller than yesterday. He could get his arms around it much more easily. And where were the crows? Edmond realized that they had not noticed him coming from a different direction. He dashed out of the grove shouting, "Crows, crows, I'm here!" When they heard him they came pouring out of their nests, swooping down toward him. "Crows!" Edmond shouted. "I have been far away."

"Cor-away!" they cried.

As Edmond hurried up the path to the farm, the crows flew around in groups, calling again and again. This excited the hens, who bustled down the path to meet him. "Tchuck-away, tchuck-away," they clucked. The big rooster was there, poking his head at Edmond. He let forth a loud crow. Had Edmond really come back?

The cows clustered along the edge of the field, greeting Edmond, "Moo-way, moo-way." Ned leaned over the gate, arching his neck and tossing his head with excitement. The calves said nothing as usual, but they all lined up in front of the open barn and stared. And the sow? She was no longer alone. She had at least twelve piglets with her. She actually stood up and came forward to grunt at Edmond, and the piglets came squealing along beside her to gasp in amazement at the stranger. Edmond paused to try and count them but they scrambled around so much it was impossible. The ducks were all on their pond and paddled over quickly.

"Ducks," said Edmond, "I have been far away."

"Quack-away," they squawked back. Some came waddling out of their pond to greet him.

Then he went over to stand at the front door of the house for a moment – to stare first at all his friends and then look over toward the hill, knowing that behind it was another country. It was probably still there. He would look at it again soon.

"I have been far away!" he shouted as he turned to enter his home. "I have been far away, and I have come back."